OXFORD
UNIVERSITY PRESS

Great Clarendon Street, Oxford OX2 6DP

Oxford University Press is a department of the University of Oxford.
It furthers the University's objective of excellence in research, scholarship,
and education by publishing worldwide. Oxford is a registered trade mark of
Oxford University Press in the UK and in certain other countries

British Library Cataloguing in Publication Data

Data available

ISBN: 978-0-19-273457-0

1 3 5 7 9 10 8 6 4 2

Printed in Great Britain

Paper used in the production of this book is a natural,
recyclable product made from wood grown in sustainable forests.
The manufacturing process conforms to the environmental
regulations of the country of origin.

FOR DULCIE AND LAURENCE

PUGS
OF THE
FROZEN NORTH

Arrooooo!

BY PHILIP REEVE
AND.
SARAH MCINTYRE

OXFORD
UNIVERSITY PRESS

ONE

Winter came in the night, like a
white sheet laid over the world. It
came so cold and so fast that the waves
of the ocean froze as they rolled. The
good ship *Lucky Star* froze with them,
trapped tight in the suddenly solid sea.

Shen the cabin boy, the youngest
member of the crew, stirred in his sleep
as the sounds of rippling and splashing
faded into frozen silence. He snuggled
deeper under the covers, trying to keep
warm. Into the silence came other
noises. First, the creaking of metal as

1

the ice tightened its grip upon
the old ship's sides. Then the voice of
Captain Jeggings, bellowing, 'All hands
on deck!'

The crew bumbled blinking from their
bunks. Able Seaman Bo, Mungbean the
ship's cook, and Shen. They stumbled
out on deck and stared at the frozen
waves which reared up all around them,
stiff and white as giant meringues.

'Don't just stand there!' shouted
Captain Jeggings, hauling on an icy
rope. 'Get us out of here!'

The rope snapped in his hands with
a sound like breaking glass. The *Lucky
Star* groaned and quivered as the ice
clenched tighter.

'What shall we do?' asked Shen.

But Captain Jeggings didn't know. Nor
did Able Seaman Bo. Nor did Mungbean.
They'd weathered storms and sat out
calms, but they'd never seen a sea like
this before.

Creak. Crunch. Big tusks of ice pushed the planks apart and pierced the *Lucky Star*'s sides. *Slosh. Gurgle.* Cold black water which hadn't frozen yet came swirling in. The ship sagged, and all the icicles that decked her rigging tinkled cheerfully. But Captain Jeggings couldn't see anything to be cheerful about.

'The cargo!' he shouted. 'We must save the cargo!'

All summer long, the *Lucky Star* had been cruising from port to port, selling this and buying that. Two thousand chunky-knit jumpers from the Isles of Aran, a second-hand snowmobile—and sixty-six pugs. Captain Jeggings had said those tiny dogs would sell like hot pies. Now, down in the leaking hold, they set up a terrible howling as cold sea sloshed round their paws.

'The dogs!' shouted Shen. 'We must save the dogs!'

Mungbean and Bo went running down the steep stairways which led to the cargo holds and came struggling back up with crates of jumpers. Captain Jeggings winched the snowmobile over the ship's side. Meanwhile, Shen upended the boxes where the pugs slept. The tiny dogs raced up on deck and jumped off the *Lucky Star*'s sides on to the ice.

Shen had heard people talk about rats leaving a sinking ship before, but he'd never heard of pugs leaving a freezing one. There's a first time for everything, he thought, as he dragged the sack which held their leads up on to deck and threw it after them.

The *Lucky Star* shuddered again, squeezed in the teeth of the ice. Rivets popped out of the deck. The funnel trembled like a chopped tree.

ABANDON SHIP! WOMEN AND CAPTAINS FIRST!

shouted Captain Jeggings, jumping over the side.

But Shen had thought of something else that needed to be saved. 'The dog food! It's still on board!'

'It'll have to stay there, then!' yelled Bo, jumping down on to the ice with Mungbean. Shen passed the smallest of the pugs down to them, then jumped after them.

With a final heave, the ice crushed the old ship flat.

Shen and the pugs stood and shivered, while Captain Jeggings and the others got the snowmobile ready. Its engine coughed and snarled as they started it up. Into its trailer they piled the crates of cargo—but there was no room for the dogs.

'We can't leave them behind!' wailed Shen.

'Well, we can't stay here with them,' said Captain Jeggings. 'This ice might melt as quickly as it came, and then where would we be? Way out at sea without a ship under us. Awkward.' (He had told Shen that the sixty-six pugs would sell like hot pies, but he meant that they would sell *in* hot pies: his auntie ran a pie shop at home, and she was always looking for new ingredients. They were by far the least valuable bit of his cargo, so he had decided to leave them behind.)

'Maybe they'll follow us!' said Shen. He climbed aboard the snowmobile with Bo and Mungbean and the captain. 'Come on doggies!' he called to the pugs.

The dogs looked up at him, heads on one side. Their hot breath steamed and smouldered in the cold air like the breath of sixty-six tiny dragons.

The snowmobile set off with a roar. The tower of crates in its trailer teetered and swayed as it went weaving its way between the frozen waves.

The pugs sat where they were, and watched it go.

'Come on!' shouted Shen. But they didn't seem to understand.

'Wait for me, Captain!' he yelled, and jumped down off the snowmobile. The frozen waves were slipperier than hills of glass. He slithered over them, back to where the pugs sat, and when they saw Shen coming their tails began to wag and they ran to meet him.

'Come on, doggies!' he said, patting sixty-six small, soft heads and getting licked by sixty-six small, soft tongues. 'You've got to follow Captain Jeggings ...'

But when he turned to look for the snowmobile, it was nowhere to be seen. Either Captain Jeggings hadn't heard when Shen shouted for it to wait . . . or he had decided that Shen and sixty-six pugs weren't worth waiting for.

TWO

Shen could still hear the snowmobile's engine buzzing like a distant bee. He started after it, following the scratch marks that its tracks had left along the troughs between the waves. The pugs seemed to understand now that they were meant to come with him, and they did. But they weren't used to walking on ice. Their claws skittered and scrabbled on the frozen sea. They lost their footing and fell on their faces, or slid on their tummies down the steep sides of the stilled waves.

'This is hopeless!' said Shen, as he slithered to and fro, trying to help them. The sound of the engine was growing fainter and fainter in the distance. Soon Shen could not hear it at all. He kept following the snowmobile's tracks, while the pugs skidded after him. Big, feathery flakes of snow began to fall. It made the pugs sneeze, and covered the tracks completely.

Through the snowflakes, Shen saw something on the ice ahead. It was one of the crates from the snowmobile trailer. It had burst open, and a pile of woolly jumpers had spilled out. Shen guessed it hadn't fallen off the trailer by accident. Bo and Mungbean had always been kind to him, ever since they'd found him as a baby, adrift in an upturned umbrella in the South China Sea. They must have tried to persuade Captain Jeggings to stop and wait. When he wouldn't, they'd quietly heaved

the jumper crate on the trailer, so that
at least Shen would have something to
keep him warm.

'Thanks, Mungbean,' said Shen.
'Thanks, Bo.'

He put on a couple of the jumpers, and
looked back. The pugs were trailing
after him. They were getting better at
walking on the ice, but they were all
shivering with the cold, poor things.

Shen took out his pocket knife. Quickly, he cut the sleeves off thirty-three jumpers and made cosy Aran body-stockings for them.

As he was cramming the pugs into the sleeves, he started to notice a new sound. *Rummmble*, it went. *Rummmmble.*

At first he hoped it might be the snowmobile coming back . . .

Then he worried that the ice was cracking.

Then he realized that it was the pugs' empty tummies rumbling. No wonder they were going so slowly! They weren't just cold and frightened—they were hungry!

They sat there sadly in their new jumpers, tails down, ears drooping, waiting for their breakfast.

Shen scrambled to the top of a frozen wave and looked around. Through the snow, he saw a dark line of cliffs not far off.

The waves must have hidden it from Captain Jeggings and the others. They would not have seen the lonely lights which twinkled there.

'Wait here!' he told the pugs.

'I'm going to fetch help!'
He spread some of the
armless jumpers on the
snow, and the pugs piled on
to them, snuggling together
in a big heap.

He laid more jumpers
over them, and told
them that he would
soon be back.
Then he set off
across the motionless
ocean.

THREE

It was hard work walking on that frozen
sea. In places the ice creaked alarmingly
and Shen had to back away and find a
different route for fear it might not take
his weight. In others it was as solid
and as clear as thick glass. He brushed
away the snow and looked down into
cold, gleaming depths where fish hung
imprisoned. Captain Jeggings had been
right about one thing. Surely there had
never been a winter like this before!

As Shen reached the shore, the sun came up, peeking nervously over the edge of the icy world and scattering sequins on the snow. It shone on the frozen fjord which lay between the cliffs. It cast long shadows from the spindly legs of the houses which perched on stilts along the fjord's edge. Smoke was drifting from their tin chimneys. Shen thought they were the cosiest, funniest-looking houses he had ever seen. How nice it must be, to live in a house on stilts! He ran up the frozen beach towards the nearest.

26

A girl no older than Shen was
sweeping snow off the front step. Above
the door some letters had been nailed
to the wooden wall. They spelled out a
mysterious message.

PO OF ICE

'What's a "Po of ice"?' asked Shen.

The girl looked up. She had a round face, and her cheeks were rosy with the effort of sweeping. 'It's meant to say Post Office,' she said. 'But the S and the T blew away. Also one of the Fs.' She tossed her broom aside and held out a small, mittened hand for Shen to shake. 'I'm Sika. Who are you?'

'I'm Shen,' said Shen. 'I've been shipwrecked. Oh, please, I need help, and dog food!'

Sika frowned. She had thick black eyebrows like lines drawn with charcoal. They were very good for frowning with. 'You have dogs?'

'Yes! They are waiting out on the ice! I have to get them to shore quickly, before the ice melts!'

'Oh, it won't melt!' said Sika. 'Don't you know what this is? Didn't you notice how suddenly the cold came? This is no ordinary winter. This is a magical winter. A once-in-a-lifetime winter. My grandpa has told me about winters like this. That ice won't melt till spring. But tell me about your dogs. How many do you have?'

'Sixty-six,' said Shen.

'Sixty-six!'

'Yes. So I'm afraid they'll need quite a lot of food, and I don't have any money ...'

Sika was looking at him, and her eyes were sparkling just as brightly as the sunlit snow. 'Never mind money! If I give you some dog food, could I have some of your dogs?'

Shen shrugged. He hadn't really thought yet about what he was going to do with the sixty-six pugs. He supposed he couldn't keep them. Not all of them, anyway. And this Po of Ice looked like the sort of place where pugs might be happy. 'Yes,' he said.

Sika turned and ran inside the Po of Ice. Shen had a glimpse through the door as it closed behind her. It was snug and cluttered inside, and he saw shelves with tins of soup and racks of tools, and big bins labelled PORRIDGE and TREACLE. The Po of Ice wasn't just a post office, it was a general store as well, but it didn't look as if it was a very busy one.

'Ma! Grandpa!' he could hear Sika shouting. 'I'm going to help a boy who's been shipwrecked! He has dogs! He's going to give us some!'

A moment later she came slamming back out, carrying a bin nearly as big as she was. This one was labelled DOG FOOD.

'Come on,' she said. 'We'll use Grandpa's sled to get it out to your camp on the ice.'

Shen helped her carry the dog food bin round the side of the Po of Ice, to a shed.

When Sika booted the door open, the pale snow-light shone in and showed Shen a strange shape. As his eyes grew accustomed to the dim light, Shen saw that it was a magnificent sled, with sleek whalebone runners.

'I've never seen a sled like that!' he gasped.

'Grandpa built this sled when he was a boy,' said Sika. 'But we don't have a dog team to pull it any more. That's why I'm so glad you showed up! Just in time, too! On the first day of True Winter!'

Shen wasn't quite sure what she meant.

'So, if you don't have any dogs to pull it,' he said, 'how are we going to get it out on to the ice?'

Sika did an eyebrow thing at him, as if to ask, how stupid are you?

'We're going to push it, of course!' she said.

34

FOUR

Up the steep slope behind the Po of Ice they went, puffing and panting, pushing the heavy sled ahead of them. They soon grew hot, despite the cold. Sika pulled off her mittens and hat and let the snowflakes settle in her hair.

But it was all worth it when they reached the top of the headland. From there they could see the pugs, out on the ice. The heap of little dogs under their coverlet of jumpers looked like a knitted tent from that distance.

They climbed on to the sled beside
the dog food bin, and Sika pushed off.
The sled went swooshing down the
headland's flank. Its runners threw up
great fans of powdered snow as Sika
leaned this way and that to steer it
around rocks and frozen bushes which
loomed up in its path.

'Wheeeee!' she shouted.

'Waaaaaargh!' screamed Shen.

The cliffs at the headland's edge were drawing closer.

But Sika knew the headland well, and she had aimed the sled at the place where the cliffs were lowest. They weren't really cliffs at all, more like a stony step, and the sled shot over it, landed with a thump on the sea-ice, and kept going, slithering between the frozen waves almost all the way to the camp.

The heap of pugs heard them coming. Sixty-six small specks bounced and yapped upon the ice, wagging their wiry tails in welcome.

'There are the dogs!' said Shen.

'Where?' asked Sika, looking around. 'Those? Those are dogs?'

The pugs had caught the scent of dog food. They crowded round the sled, yipping and whining, wagging their tails. Shen opened the dog food bin and shovelled out scoopfuls of kibble. Soon the yapping was replaced by crunching.

Shen looked around at them happily. Then he looked behind him. Sika was sitting on the sled. She had her head in her hands, and she was crying.

'What's the matter?' he asked.

'Oomph!' went Sika. Tears trickled down her face and dripped off her chin and froze before they hit the ice, where they landed with tiny plinking sounds. 'Oomph!' she said. 'When you said you had sixty-six dogs, I thought you meant proper ones!'

'These are proper ones!' said Shen.

'No they're not! They couldn't pull a sled!'

'Oh!' said Shen. Now he understood. So that was why she had wanted some of his dogs. He looked at the sled; the bigness of it. It needed a team of huskies to tow it, not a team of pugs.

'I thought Grandpa could enter the race after all!' sniffled Sika. 'And now I shall have to go home and tell him it's hopeless.'

'What race?' asked Shen.

'The Great Northern Race,' said Sika miserably. 'When True Winter comes, the teams arrive from all over the north. They will race through the night-forests and across the frozen sea, all the way to the Snowfather's palace at the top of the world.'

Shen scratched his head. He remembered the charts he'd seen on board the *Lucky Star*. The North Pole was just a patch of bare paper so big and white it made him want to get a pencil out and draw something, anything on it. 'There isn't any palace at the top of the world,' he said.

'There is if it's a True Winter,' said Sika. 'That's where the Snowfather lives. And he grants the wish of the first adventurer to reach it.' She sighed.

'Grandpa almost won it once, when he was not much older than me. Such stories he tells about that journey! And he's waited and waited for True Winter to return, ever since. He kept this sled, and bred the best team of sled-dogs in the north. But True Winter comes only once in a lifetime. The dogs got old and died, and Grandpa got old too, and soon he'll die. And now True Winter is here at last, and when you said dogs I thought you meant proper dogs, I thought Grandpa would be able to race after all, and I'd go with him to the North Pole and see the Snowfather. But these are just toy dogs.'

'No they're not!' said Shen. 'Just because they're tiny, it doesn't mean they're not strong, and loyal, and brave. And I have leads for all of them. I bet they could pull you and your Grandpa all the way to the North Pole easily!'

Sika didn't look as if she believed him, so he ran and fetched the sack of leads which was still lying on the ice where the *Lucky Star* had gone down. He rushed back and started clipping the leads to the pugs' jumpers and knotting the other ends to Sika's sled. (He was very good at knots, having grown up on a ship.)

The pugs caught his excitement and started to yip and yap and dance around, straining and pulling at the heavy thing he'd hitched them to.

Ten pugs couldn't shift the sled at all. Twenty couldn't. Even when thirty were attached, it didn't budge, and Sika said, 'See? They just aren't sled-dogs. This is hopeless.'

But when forty dogs were tied on, the big sled stirred, and slid a few inches over the ice. When fifty were attached, it started to gather speed. When the sixty-sixth was in position, Sika shouted, 'Mush, doggies! Mush!' and it shot away as speedily as any normal, huskie-

powered sled. It whizzed over the frozen
waves, throwing up fans of powdered
ice each time it turned. The pugs were
getting used to running on ice. They
kept tumbling over each other and
getting their leads in a tangle at first,
but they soon sorted themselves out, and
by the time Sika had circled the pile of
jumpers six times the sled was running
straight and true.

She grinned at Shen, her face all rosy
with cold and happiness. 'It must be the
best sled ever! Can I really take your
tiny dogs to the North Pole?'

Shen felt a bit unsure about that. He
hadn't meant to give her all the pugs. He
was going to miss them. But Sika had
saved them, and he didn't want to make
her cry again, so he said, 'All right . . .'

'I can't wait to tell Grandpa!' she said.
And she took a spare lead and cracked it
in the air above the pugs' tiny heads like
a whip.

Two hundred and sixty-four tiny paws pattered on the ice, sixty-six little voices howled 'AROOO!' and the sled set off, back towards the land.

FIVE

Once they had made the sled-shed into a kennel for the pugs, Shen followed Sika inside. It was cosy in the Po of Ice, warmed by the heat from a stove. A woman was heating milk in a pan. She had the same charcoal eyebrows as Sika, and the same wide smile. 'Sika!' she said, 'you must be frozen! Did you find your dogs?'

'Yes, Mum!' said Sika.

'And this must be your shipwrecked friend,' said Sika's mum. 'Poor boy! Is there anyone we can contact for you?'

'Not really,' said Shen.

'Well,' said Sika's mother, 'I shall make breakfast for you both.'

Sika led him round behind the counter, into a back room where a big, carved bed stood. In the bed, beneath a mound of furs and quilted counterpanes, lay the biggest man Shen had ever seen.

He was so big that Shen wasn't even sure he *was* a man at first; under all those coverings he looked like an old boat which had been brought ashore and turned upside down for winter. Then Shen saw the big, bearded face resting on the pillows, and realized that the rumbling sound he could hear was snores.

'That's Grandpa,' whispered Sika.

The old man's face was grey with age, rugged as a mountain rock. Shen remembered Sika saying that her grandpa would soon die, and wondered if he was going to do it now. But then beneath one bushy eyebrow a bright eye opened and turned to stare at Shen.

'Grandpa, this is Shen,' Sika said. 'He was shipwrecked, and he has dogs with him! We can enter the race!'

'Ah,' said the old man, 'So Sika has told you about the race?'

'A bit,' said Shen.

'It did not always used to be a race,' said Grandpa, in his deep, rumbly voice. 'In the olden days, no one knew of the Snowfather or his icicle palace. Then, one True Winter, a brave girl named Ooka strapped on her skis and went exploring. Fifty kinds of snow she met. She crossed Kraken Deep, but the Kraken was sleeping, and did not trouble her. All the way to the top of the world she went, and when she got there she found the old Snowfather waiting, and he granted her a wish.'

Just then, Sika's mum granted Shen's wish, with a mug of hot chocolate and hot waffles with honey. Grandpa went on.

'Well, of course, Ooka's story spread far and wide. One lifetime later, when another True Winter turned the sea to ice, all the brave young men of the north went racing off to see if they could get their wishes granted too. "Oh no," said the Snowfather. "Do you know how hard it is to make wishes come true? Only the one who was first to reach me shall have their wish granted!" And he sent the rest home disappointed.

'Well, after that, each time True Winter dawned, there were all sorts of fights and rages, everyone trying to be the first to reach the Snowfather. "We can't have this," he said, seeing the blood on the snow as young warriors fought each other to be first through the gates of his palace. "There must be rules! There must be fairness! You must all start together, and the best sled will win."

'And that is why, ever since, all those who seek the Snowfather's palace set out together, from Snowdovia. That is where I started from, the year I made the trip . . .'

The wind was rising outside. The thin hissing it made must have sounded to Grandpa like runners racing over snow. He closed his eyes and smiled, imagining his bed was a sled, carrying him north.

'Tell us more!' said Sika. 'Tell us about Kraken Deep and the Lost Hope!'

Grandpa shook his head. 'I don't remember those stories any more,' he said. 'It was all so long ago. True Winter comes but once in a lifetime, and I have seen two, which means my lifetime must be over. I wish I could see the old Snowfather one more time, but I am too old now to make the journey. My time is nearly done.'

'Oh Grandpa!' said Sika, and Shen thought that she was going to cry again. 'Maybe we can take you! You've waited so long!'

'No, Sika,' he said. 'But you should go.'

'Me?' said Sika.

'All on her own?' said Sika's mother worriedly.

'I'll come too!' said Shen. After all, he thought, it wasn't as if he had anything better to do, now that the *Lucky Star* was sunk and Captain Jeggings had abandoned him.

'Yes,' said Grandpa. 'You should both go! You mustn't miss a chance like this! You're young and brave, and the carvings on my sled will keep away the trolls and snowspooks and other creatures which wander abroad in a True Winter. And when you see the Snowfather, tell him I send my regards.'

'I'll do better than that,' said Sika. 'I'll ask him to make you well again, and then you'll remember all the stories, and live to see a third True Winter, probably.'

'All that way, with only such little

dogs to pull you?' said Sika's mother doubtfully. But she had been listening to Grandpa's stories of the Great North Race all her life, just like Sika had. If she hadn't had to stay and look after him, she would have been jumping on that sled herself.

From outside there came a sound like wild applause. Fireworks were blooming above the frozen hills.

'That is the race-meet beginning, down at Snowdovia,' said Sika.

Her grandpa reached out his arms and took Shen's and Sika's hands in his. 'Good luck!' he whispered. 'And now you must go! The race will soon be starting!'

SIX

The town of Snowdovia was built in the same style as the Po of Ice, on stilted platforms along a fjord-edge. But unlike the Po of Ice, it was full of life and bustle. People lined the balconies outside their homes to watch as the adventurers who meant to race to the top of the world came sledding into their fjord.

From all over the north they came. True Winter had not arrived completely without warning. Not for people who knew what to look for. Not for people who had been eagerly waiting for the first flake of magical snow to fall. They had been preparing for weeks, and now that the ice had come, they were ready.

At Limpetville Institute of Technology, Professor Shackleton Jones had known about the coming winter by the excited way the Northern Lights made his particle detectors ping. He was determined to reach the top of the world using the power of Science. He and his robot companion SNOBOT swept into Snowdovia on a carbon-fibre sled so strong and lightweight that it was barely there at all.

On a lonely island not far from Snowdovia, Helga Hammerfest had learned of the big freeze by watching the flight of geese and the way the spiders spun their cobwebs. She had readied her sled, and harnessed up her team—

no dogs for Helga, just her two pet
polar bears, Snowdrop and Slushpuppy.
She was the local favourite, so she got
an extra big cheer when her snow-bears
came lumbering up to the starting line.
  Sir Basil Sprout-Dumpling heard of the
freeze from his butler, Sideplate, who
had been keeping watch on the weather

forecasts. Ten minutes later they were at the airport, loading Sir Basil's sled and pedigree dog team aboard an aeroplane. Sir Basil's father had been the first to reach the top of the world last time True Winter came. He had met the Snowfather, and had his wish granted, which was to be ridiculously rich. He had gone back to England with a fortune in rubies, sapphires and diamonds, but Sir Basil had spent it all. 'If we don't beat these riff-raff to the Pole, Sideplate,' he said as they drew up to the starting line, 'I shall have to sell off the old stately home. I mean to win this race, even if I have to cheat like an absolute bounder.'

'Yes, Sir Basil,' said Sideplate sadly, holding his bowler hat on tight and wishing he'd worn warmer underwear. 'But if I may say so, Sir Basil, I do hope cheating won't be necessary.' Sir Basil wasn't listening. 'I say!' he cried. For the pink sled that had just pulled up next to him held none other than Mitzi Von Primm, most glamorous of all the racers. How embarrassed her team of huskies looked, clipped like poodles and dyed pink to match Mitzi's stylish racing outfit!

Those four were not the only entrants for the race. There were dozens of others: modern sleds with sat-nav and central heating, age-old sleds of wood and bone, a sled folded out of stiff paper by an Origami master from Japan, and an inflatable sled advertising 'Poo-B-Gone' poop-scoops. There was even a sled crewed by two ladies who were doing the race for charity, dressed as a pantomime zebra. It took quite a while to get them all sorted out, and arranged along the starting line. The over-excited dogs woofed and yapped and howled and sniffed each other's bottoms and started fights. The over-excited race marshals skated to and fro, checking that nobody was cheating and no dog (or polar bear) had its nose over the line.

They had almost finished, and the Chief Marshal was just cleaning the snow out of her starting pistol and getting ready to fire it when people standing near the fjord's end began to shout, 'Wait! Wait! Here comes another!' A ripple of applause spread along the fjord side as the late arrival headed for the starting line.

'That looks like young Sika, in her grandpa's old sled,' said the Chief Marshal, scraping away the ice that had formed on the lenses of her binoculars. 'But what are those little woolly things pulling it?'

'They look like sixty-six pugs,' said her assistant.

'Pugs?' said the Chief Marshal.

'Pugs?' said the other racers, turning to stare as Sika steered the old sled into a gap between Sir Basil's and Mitzi Von Primm's, and Shen reined in the eager little dogs.

'I say!' complained Sir Basil, as the marshals came skating over to take the names of the new arrivals. 'They've got sixty-six dogs! That's against all the rules!'

'And those dogs are wearing woolly jumpers,' agreed Mitzi. 'I'm not sure that's allowed.'

But Helga Hammerfest, whose sled was on the other side of Mitzi's, said, 'Well, dear, your huskies are dyed pink and have ribbons in their fur. I don't think you'll find that mentioned in the rulebook, either.'

(Mitzi blushed, and her poor pink dogs all hung their heads in shame.)

'And Shackleton Jones's sled is pulled by robot dogs!' Helga pointed out.

'These are Woof-O-Tron 2000s, my very latest invention,' said Shackleton Jones, proudly.

'And those sixty-six little dogs are each about a tenth of the size of one of yours, Sir Basil,' Helga went on. 'And you've got eight, so you've got more dog power than these youngsters. What's the matter? Afraid that smart sled of yours won't be as fast as their antique?'

'Of course not!' said Sir Basil, but he didn't say it very loudly, because Helga was half as tall again as him, and twice as wide, and he didn't fancy getting into an argument with her (also, her polar bears kept giving him very nasty looks).

So the Chief Marshal wrote Shen and Sika's names on her clipboard, and stepped into the little balloon that was waiting on the fjord side to carry her up above the starting line.

Shen and Sika had left the Po of Ice in a terrible hurry, having quickly packed the sled with supplies for themselves and the pugs. All the way to Snowdovia they had been worrying that they would be too late. Now Sika turned to Shen and beamed. 'We did it!'

Shen was not so sure. They were in the race, but that was only the beginning. How could they hope to win it, when the other sleds looked so speedy,

and the other dogs so big and strong.
Still, it would be something just to
start. The sound of all the dogs filled
the frosty air, and made him feel eager
to be off. He waved at Helga and said,
'Thank you, sir!'

'She's a lady!' hissed Sika.

'Is she?' asked Shen.

'I am,' said
Helga Hammerfest.
'But don't worry,
I am always getting
mistaken for a man,

on account of my size, and also my beard. Most ladies don't care for beards, but I find mine helps to keeps my chin warm in the frozen north. You should try growing yours, Miss Mitzi.'

Mitzi Von Primm shuddered. 'My fur-lined racing coat is all I need to keep me warm,' she said. 'It's by a very good designer, you know.'

The Chief Marshal interrupted, drifting above them in her balloon and shouting through a huge megaphone. Her words boomed across the ice, and broken bits of them came bouncing back from the frozen hillsides.

'Welcome to the Great Northern Race! Now, you all know the course! North, through the Night Forest, then over Kraken Deep, and then by whatever route you want to the palace at the top of the world. Good luck! Give our regards to the Snowfather! And may the best sled win!'

Then she fired her starting pistol. The
racers cracked their whips and hollered
at their dogs, and the sleds set off,
rushing across the ice.

There were some disasters right away, which was only to be expected with so many sleds all starting out together. Some tangled in each other's runners. Some of the dog-packs stopped running and started fighting. A speedy Russian sled crashed nose-first into a hole which opened suddenly in the ice (Sir Basil chuckled and tossed away a can of anti-freeze).

A small avalanche, triggered by all the noise, came rushing down the fjord side and crumpled the origami sled before it had gone ten metres.

The inflatable sled popped when one
of the dogs pulling the sled behind it
mistook it for a huge runaway sausage
and took a bite. And three sleds were
knocked over when the Chief Marshal's
balloon fell on top of them—she had
accidentally punctured it when she fired
the starting pistol.

But the others were away. Shackleton Jones was in the lead, with Sir Basil close behind, until Mitzi Von Primm took a daring shortcut between two ragged rocks and overtook them both. Helga's polar bears galloped lazily along, not bothering to go too fast yet. And right at the back, pulled by their sixty-six panting pugs, came Shen and Sika.

'It's no good!' shouted Shen, clinging on tight as they left the smooth ice of the fjord and started bounding and bouncing over snowy ground. 'They'll be at the top of the world long before us!'

'Maybe not,' said Sika. 'It's not just about being fast. It's about luck! It will take at least a week to reach the North Pole. All sorts of things will happen on the way! What will you wish for if you get there first? What's your heart's desire, Shen?'

'I don't know,' said Shen. He had
been thinking about it a lot, as the sled
whisked along. He supposed he ought to
wish for a family. He had never had one
of his own, except for Bo and Mungbean
and Captain Jeggings, who didn't really
count. But he didn't want a magic family,
just an ordinary one. So he said, 'I'm still
thinking about it.'

'I know exactly what I want,' said
Sika. 'I'll ask the Snowfather to make
Grandpa well again. To let him live
another lifetime, so he'll have a chance
to race again next time True Winter
comes.'

'Can the Snowfather really do that?'
wondered Shen.

'Of course he can! He can do anything!'

Shen looked back, and wished
that he knew what to wish for. He
saw that the fjord and the starting
line had already fallen far behind.

Zzzzzzzssssssssssszzzzssss went the runners, racing over snow and ice. HoooooOOOOOoOOOoOoOO went the wind, whistling around the sled. And the sixty-six pugs went . . .

YIP YIP YIP
YIP YIP YIP YIP
YIP YIP YIP YIP YI
YIP YIP YIP
YIP
YIP YIP YIP YIP
YIP YIP
YIP

SEVEN

They rushed into the Night Forest,
following the tracks of the sleds that had
gone ahead of them, weaving between
the tall, dark trees. Far ahead, they could
sometimes hear the deep barking of
other sled teams, and the pugs lifted up
their little heads and answered: YIP YIP
YIP! They were loving it. They felt like
real dogs at last, the sort of dogs that
they were in their secret doggy dreams.

But all that woofing and yipping
made the dark trees tremble, and down
from the branches slid great dollops of

snow—*FLUMP,
FLUMP, FLUMP.*
Somehow,
Sika steered her way
around them without
crashing into any tree-
trunks. Other sleds were
not so fortunate. They passed
two which had been smashed
by the snow-flumps, and whose
grumpy owners were starting
the long walk back to Snowdovia.
And near the far edge of the forest
they found Shackleton Jones standing

under the trees, watching while SNOBOT dug his hi-tech sled and robot dog-team out of a massive snow-dollop. Sika slowed her sled to ask if he needed help, but he just grinned and said, 'I have all the help I need! SNOBOT is designed to dig a tonne of snow per minute! You'll soon have us out of here, won't you, SNOBOT?' He beamed at the children again. 'So, kids! Next stop, Kraken's Deep, eh. What's supposed to go on there, do you think?'

'They say the Kraken sleeps there,' said Sika. 'It's this ancient sea monster with tentacles and things. When True Winter comes it rises to the surface. If we're lucky, the ice will be thick enough to stop it reaching up and grabbing us.'

Shackleton Jones laughed. 'The Kraken? You don't believe in that old story, do you? It's just a legend of the sea, like the Bermuda Triangle, or the Night of the Seawigs.'

'Idiot,' muttered Sika, as they went on. 'He'll be saying next that the Snowfather himself is just a legend.'

'At least we're not the last any more!' said Shen, looking back over his shoulder as they left the snow-flumped sled behind. But secretly he was hoping that Shackleton Jones had been right about the Kraken.

They shot out of the forest and went swooshing down a long, smooth slope. They left the land and went speeding over the sea. The ice was smoother here. It was sheltered by high, dark, rocks, which poked from the frozen sea in a wide ring. It was as smooth as a skating rink, and all over its surface Shen could see the tracks of the other sleds which had come this way, heading towards the north.

'What a strange place!' he said. 'I wonder if the Kraken really does live here?'

He looked down. The frozen sea was as clear as glass—thick and ripply, like the glass in front doors. He looked down through it, and from the cold depths, something looked up at him.

The sled was hurtling above an eye the size of a car park.

And all those snaky rocks weren't rocks at all - they were the tips of massive tentacles, frozen as the Kraken lifted them up out of the sea.

'Er—Sika?' said Shen.

'What is it?'

Shen looked down at the eye again. He was sure that it was staring right at him. And then, as he stared back at it, it blinked.

Crack—crash! The towering tentacles twitched. Cascades of shattered ice came raining down their sides like broken glass as the tips waved, trying to break free and snatch at Shen and Sika. Cracks spread across the ice.

'Go faster!' Shen shouted.

But the sixty-six pugs were already running as fast as they could. Their little pink tongues were hanging out, and their hot breath made plumes of steam in the icy air. Their paws skittered on the frozen sea. A crack went zig-zagging across the ice in front of them and they jumped it, the sled bumping behind them. Then another. The pugs veered away as the crack widened, but now more cracks were opening all around.

The ice of Kraken's Deep jumped like a drumskin as the huge beast beneath it lurched upwards, and all the tentacles writhed and strained.

The pugs stopped running. There was nowhere to run to; the sled was on an icy island, surrounded by widening cracks. The island began to tilt, and the sled slithered backwards. Quickly, Shen leaned over the front of the sled and began unclipping the pugs's leads. If it slid right over the edge of the ice and down into the dark water, he did not want it to drag all the poor pugs with it.

With a terrible splintering noise, one of the Kraken's tentacles tore free of the ice and came groping towards the stranded sled, showering Shen and Sika with cold salt water and shards of ice which smashed all around them like dropped window panes. The Kraken's huge eye watched coldly from below. It had been asleep for a long time—ever since the last True Winter, in fact. The runners of all the other sleds had woken it as they went skreeling across the ice. Now it was looking for its breakfast.

But the pugs were not having any of that. They began to yip and yap even louder than before. They bounced about on their short legs, barking and snarling at the huge purple tentacle as it curled above them. One, braver than the rest, bounced so high that he managed to sink his teeth into the tip of it. The startled Kraken lashed its tentacle about, but the pug clung on tight. All the other pugs thought that looked such fun that they went charging off to find tentacles of their own to attack. Without the heavy sled to pull they jumped easily over the cracks the Kraken had opened.

Yipping fiercely, they
flung themselves at
the twining tentacles
and bit them, hard.

The Kraken thrashed about, trying to shake them off, but they just wagged their tails and snarled. The huge creature stared up through the ice in confusion. It had fought battles with killer whales in the dark blue depths, and dragged polar bears down into its chilly lair, but it had never met creatures like these before. Little specks, like flakes of wind-blown fluff . . . But fluff with teeth!

Ow! thought the Kraken. And one by one it snaked its tentacles back down into the deep. The pugs let go as the tentacle-tips vanished back beneath the ice, but they kept barking and snarling and yipping.

Shen and Sika stared down through the ice. The great eye of the Kraken stared angrily back for a moment. Then it vanished, as the Kraken squirted out a huge black cloud of ink to hide itself.

When the ink cleared, the Kraken was

gone. It had swum away to find a less dangerous breakfast—maybe a shark or two, out in the deep ocean. In the holes and cracks which it had made, the water was already freezing again.

'Phew!' said Shen, and started gathering the pugs together again.

'Wait until I tell Grandpa!' said Sika. 'That was as good as any of his stories!'

For the first time, Shen felt that there was a chance they might win. Then, while they were busy reattaching the pugs to the sled, they heard the barking of another dog team behind them. Shackleton Jones and SNOBOT had got their sled working again, and they came swooping across Kraken's Deep, waving as they zipped past Shen and Sika.

'See?' shouted Shackleton Jones. 'There's no Kraken here! It's all just a silly superstition!'

'But . . .' Shen started to say.

It was no use. Already Shackleton

94

Jones and his sled were just a dot, dwindling into the north.

'Great,' said Sika. 'Now we're last again!'

'But we have the bravest dog team,' said Shen, scattering doggy treats for the pugs.

EIGHT

All through the night and all through
the following day the race ran on,
and all sorts of adventures . . . and
accidents . . . befell the other sleds.

Before long there were only five sleds left. Sir Basil Sprout-Dumpling was in the lead, thanks to a map his father had drawn which showed shortcuts between the rocks and islands of the frozen sea. But Helga Hammerfest was not far behind, and Mitzi Von Primm and Shackleton Jones were catching up fast. (Shen and Sika were right at the back, of course, so far behind that the others didn't even know they were still in the race.)

On the third night, when Sideplate stopped the sled, Sir Basil could hear the baying of Mitzi's team behind him. It sounded as though she had overtaken Helga Hammerfest.

'Those blighters are going to catch us up, Sideplate!' he complained.

'Our lead does appear to be narrowing, sir,' agreed Sideplate.

Sir Basil rubbed his mittens together gleefully. 'Well, we'll soon get rid of them! Time for Operation Detour!'

'Are you sure that's necessary, sir?' asked Sideplate.

'Of course it is! If I don't make it to the Snowfather first, my fortune is finished! Get to work!'

Sideplate sighed, and did as he was told. Out of the bundles at the front of Sir Basil's sled he fetched an inflatable signpost, which he pumped up with a bicycle pump.

'There!' said Sir Basil. 'That should get rid of the others. You know where that will take them, Sideplate?'

'No, sir.'

'Of course you don't! That's because I've been studying my father's map and you haven't. It will lead them straight to the Lost Hope. Daddy saw it from a distance when he came this way all those years ago. He told me all about it. A few of the other competitors went to have a closer look, and they were never seen again!'

'How troubling, sir.'

'Not for us it's not! The more of that shower we can get rid of, the easier we'll win. Come on, Sideplate—onwards to the Pole!'

'Very good, sir,' said Sideplate unhappily. He turned on the small portable snow-machine on the back of Sir Basil's sled. White flakes covered their tracks as they sped away.

The sign stood where they had left it. Soon, Mitzi Von Primm's sled came speeding up, turned sharp left, and followed Sir Basil's detour. Close behind came Helga Hammerfest, who also turned left. Then, a little later, Shackleton Jones arrived.

'Thin ice, eh?' he said. 'Better take the detour, SNOBOT.'

'I am not detecting thin ice ahead,' said the robot. 'It is safe to proceed due north.'

GREAT PERIL!

THIN ICE AHEAD!

PROBABLY OTHER SCARY THINGS TOO

DANGER

'Hmm. Still, better not take any chances, eh?'

After that, it was very quiet for a long time. The night grew colder and colder. It grew so cold that pieces of the Northern Lights froze and fell out of the sky. They lay strewn about on the ice, glowing gently.

At last, Shen and Sika arrived at the detour sign.

If Sika had been driving, she would

DETOUR

have known at once that the detour was a trick. Her Grandpa had told her enough stories of his race that she knew there was no such thing as thin ice, not that far north, not in a True Winter.

But Sika was not driving. Sika was asleep, wrapped up in furs, leaning against the dog food bin. And when Shen saw the signs, he turned left at once, following the tracks of all the other sleds.

The paws of the scampering pugs threw up a mist of powdered ice. It blew into Sika's sleeping face and woke her. She saw the big, gold moon, lying on the horizon far ahead, and knew at once that they were going the wrong way.

'Why have we turned?'

Shen explained.

'That can't be right!' she said. 'We must turn back!'

Shen tried to turn the sled. But by then the pugs were moving more and more slowly. That last burst of speed which woke Sika had tired them out. The sled came slowly to a halt, and the little dogs flopped down in sleepy heaps.

'We can't go any further tonight,' said Shen.

He got down from the sled and started to get food for the dogs. While they ate it, he and Sika put up Grandpa's old tent. They hammered the iron tent pegs deep into the ice in case a storm blew up while they were sleeping.

When they had all had something to eat, Shen and Sika crawled inside the tent and called the dogs in after them. They snuggled down in their sleeping bags, the sleepy pugs piled over them, and in a short time Shen was sleeping too.

But Sika could not sleep. She lay and looked at the embroidered patterns on the walls of the tent. A fallen Northern Light had wedged in a snowdrift nearby and its glow came gently through the canvas. And from somewhere not so nearby, very faintly through the frozen air, came singing.

Sika slid out from under her coverlet of pugs (they were so fast asleep that they did not notice her leaving). She went outside into the glowing night, and started walking towards the sound of the singing. If she had looked behind her as she walked, she would have seen that her footprints were quietly closing up, leaving the snow behind her smooth and white as empty pages. (There are fifty different types of snow in a True Winter, and this was blindsnow—the type that hides all tracks.)

But Sika was not looking behind her. She kept her eyes on a jaggedy hill of shattered rock ahead. (It would have been an island if the sea had been water instead of ice.) It seemed to her that the singing was coming from behind it. A green glow shone from behind it, too, as if a really big bit of the Northern Lights had fallen there.

She scrambled up between rocks and looked. There stood a huge old ship, completely trapped in the ice. The name painted on its rusty stern said, *Hope*, and suddenly Sika remembered something that her grandpa had told her, about how a lot of the teams he had raced against had got sidetracked to somewhere called 'The Lost Hope' and never been seen again.

She hadn't realized that the Lost Hope was a ship.

She went a little closer.

Parked beside the ship were three sleds. There was the hi-tech sled of Shackleton Jones, with its robot dogs waiting motionless. Next to it stood the ancient bog-oak sled of Helga Hammerfest, and Mitzi Von Primm's pink designer sled. Mitzi's dog team and Helga's polar bears snoozed beside them, but there was no sign of their owners.

Above the sleds, fragments of fallen Northern Light had been hung up along the *Hope*'s rusty side. That was where the green glow came from. The lights spelled out three words . . .

'What a strange place for a Noodle Bar,' she said to herself. 'Who would sell noodles, all the way out here?'

A huge, hairy, white hand reached out from behind a rock and grabbed her by the hood of her anorak. A huge, hairy, white voice rumbled in her ear.

'YETIS WOULD.'

NINE

No one knew how the yetis had come to
that place. Had they arrived with the
good ship *Hope* when it ran aground and
was abandoned there? Or had they come
loping across the frozen sea one True
Winter, and decided that the wreck of
the *Hope* would be a good place to live?

  As for what had given them the idea to
open a Noodle Bar—well, that was easy.
There are fifty different types of snow
in a True Winter, and the type which
fell on that island was a very special
type, which could be made into beautiful

noodles. (It made very nice spaghetti, too, but the yetis had decided that YETI SPAGHETTI BAR sounded too obvious.)

At first, Sika was a bit frightened at being captured by a yeti, but when she realized that it only wanted her to come and eat some noodles, she calmed down. She quite liked noodles. The yeti took her by the hand and led her across the snow towards the ship. It was quite a large yeti and looked very yeti-ish, with long white hair, big feet, glowing eyes— you know the type of thing. As she followed it up the side of the ship, Sika wondered if she should tell it that Shen was nearby, and ask it if she could go and fetch him so that he could have some noodles too. Then she decided to wait until she had tried them herself. They might be horrible, and nobody likes to be woken up in the middle of the night for horrible noodles.

The decks of the *Hope* were glassy with ice, but down inside, in the old ballroom, there was warmth and light. Candles made from yeti earwax flickered there, and a yeti-dung fire burned merrily in a pudding-shaped stove. A long table had been set up in the middle of the ballroom. There sat Mitzi Von Primm, Helga Hammerfest, Shackleton Jones, and a whole load of yetis, all tucking into big bowls of snow-noodles, while yetis wearing flowery aprons carried yet more noodles in through the swing doors which led to the kitchens. These doors had round glass windows in them, and Sika peeked through as her yeti dragged her past them. She saw yetis shovelling snow out of big buckets, while others packed it into fat snowballs and stuffed them into a mincing machine. They all took turns to turn the handle of the machine, and the long white noodles came writing out of it like worms. And as the yetis worked, they sang:

Sika's yeti pulled out a chair for her, and sat her down between Mitzi Von Primm and Shackleton Jones. From the far end of the table Helga Hammerfest called, 'Yoo hoo! Welcome to the Lost Hope, Sika! You must try these noodles!'

'They're delicious!' agreed Mitzi Von Primm. 'But I mustn't have any more, I'm watching my figure.'

'Delicious indeed!' agreed Shackleton Jones. 'But I'd best be on my way. I still mean to beat you good people to the top of the world!'

But just then a yeti plonked a big dish of noodles down on the table and Mitzi and Shackleton took huge helpings for themselves, just like everybody else. Sika took some too. She was surprised how nice they tasted. She had expected them to be a bit—well—snowy, but they weren't; they were hot and nutty and delicious.

For a little while the only sounds in the old ship were of people and yetis chewing and swallowing and going, 'Mmmm.' Oh, and one other sound—a small, urgent buzzing, like a very polite alarm clock.

'Something's wrong,' said SNOBOT, looking up at Sika from under the table. 'These noodles are a bit too more-ish. That twit Shackleton's been here for hours now, eating and eating them. It's as if he's forgotten all about reaching the top of the world. And he doesn't even like noodles!'

Sika thought about that. It did sound as if something strange was going on, but it was hard to work out what, because the noodles tasted so lovely that they kept distracting her.

'These are MIND CONTROLLING NOODLES!' SNOBOT was saying. 'The yetis mean to keep you all here as their slaves!'

'Mmmm,' said Sika, helping herself to some more noodles. And then, suddenly, all the noodles were gone!

'More noodles!' roared the yetis at the table, and their human guests all joined in. 'More noodles!'

'Just coming,' said one of the yeti chefs, gathering up their empty bowls, the dirty forks and spoons and chopsticks. 'But first, you travellers must pay for the noodles you've already eaten.'

'What?' cried Mitzi. 'You never said anything about paying . . .'

'You didn't think they'd be free, did you?' growled the yetis. 'The sign outside says NOODLE BAR, not FREE NOODLES.'

'Do you take major credit cards?' asked Shackleton Jones.

'Cash only,' said the yeti chef, and the other yetis rose to their feet and looked down menacingly at their guests, who suddenly felt very small and a little frightened and yet, at the same time, still hungry for more noodles.

'If they can't pay,' said one of the yetis, 'there's only one thing for it. They're going to have to do . . . the washing up!'

He kicked open the double doors into

the kitchen. The last time she peeked in, Sika had been too interested by the snow-into-noodles machine to notice much else. Now she saw that the far side of the kitchen, where the sink was, was piled from floor to ceiling with teetering stacks of bowls, plates, jugs, saucepans, cutlery, and trays, all smeared and crusted with years of dried-on bits of noodle.

Those yetis loved making noodles, and they loved eating noodles, but they absolutely HATED washing up.

'Washing up!' they chanted, picking up their human captives and carrying them towards the kitchens. 'Washing up!'

And the humans were too full of noodles, and too afraid that the yetis might not allow them any more noodles, to resist.

So this is why no one ever returned from the Lost Hope! thought Sika, as big yeti hands lifted her out of her chair and carried her towards the kitchen. They get lured in with noodles, and then have to stay here, washing up for the rest of their lives!

She looked round and saw SNOBOT watching her. He wasn't interested in noodles, so the yetis weren't interested in him. She beckoned him closer, and while her yeti was queuing up to carry her into the kitchen after the others, she whispered quickly, 'Shen's camped not far away! Tell him not to come here! Tell him to keep going! All the way to the top of the world!'

SNOBOT whirred away. The yeti lurched into the kitchen with Sika, and the doors swung shut behind her.

TEN

Shen was back on the *Lucky Star,*
sailing homeward on a warm and sunny
evening, and all the pugs were crowding
at the ship's prow, wagging their tails
and watching for the first sight of land.
But just as he was about to tuck into the
nice fat ice cream that Captain Jeggings
had handed him, an icy breeze began to
blow. The top blew off the ice cream and
landed in Shen's face, which woke him up.

'Yuk!' and 'Brrr!' he said.

The flap of the tent was open, and SNOBOT was leaning over him. The robot was covered in snow, and a big dollop had just dropped off him and landed in Shen's face. Shen sat up, wiping it away.

'What are you doing here?' he asked. 'Where's Sika?'

SNOBOT explained.

Kidnapped by yetis?? Shen wondered if he should harness up the pugs and sled off fast, before the yetis caught him too.

But, no. Sika was his friend. She was the first proper friend he'd ever had. 'Friends don't leave friends behind to do the washing up for yetis!' he said. 'We have to do something!'

He squiggled out from under the sleepy pugs and went outside. He could hear the gruff singing of the yetis coming from behind the rocky island. He woke the pugs, and harnessed them to the sled, ready, in case he needed to make a quick getaway. With the pugs following him, he set off on foot, with SNOBOT perching on the sled as it shushed along behind them, leaving no tracks in the blindsnow.

Then they hit a patch of a different type of snow. It sang in a little squeaky voice each time Shen put his foot down, and when SNOBOT and the pugs and the sled hit it, it sounded like a snowy opera.

'Shhhh!' hissed Shen, afraid that the singing snow would warn the yetis somebody was coming.

'Shhhhh!' said a patch of snow nearby.

'Who said that?' whispered Shen.

'Who said that?' said the snow, quite loudly. It was echosnow, which repeats anything you say to it, only louder. It started all the pugs yipping, and the echosnow yipped back at them more loudly, which made the pugs yip louder still. Shen stood in a storm of yips and waited for the yetis to come and find him.

But the yetis were far too busy enjoying themselves. It was a big treat for them when newcomers arrived and they had someone else to do the washing up for a change. They had locked the doors of the kitchen and they were all outside on the deck, bathing in the green glow of the Northern Lights and singing their yeti songs.

Shen had an idea. He tiptoed over to the patch of echosnow and started clumping it into snowballs. He showed SNOBOT how to make snowballs too, and together they quickly piled the sled high with them. Then they hurried on towards the *Hope*. While SNOBOT took the sled to where the other sleds were parked and started getting them ready to leave, Shen took the snowballs and went round alone to the other side of the old ship. From there he could see the big, shaggy shapes of the yetis above him, dancing on the icy deck. He could also see a steamed-up porthole which must be the kitchen, where the washing up was happening.

Shen picked up a snowball and threw it as hard as he could up at the yetis. It was a brilliant shot, and it hit the biggest yeti right in the face.

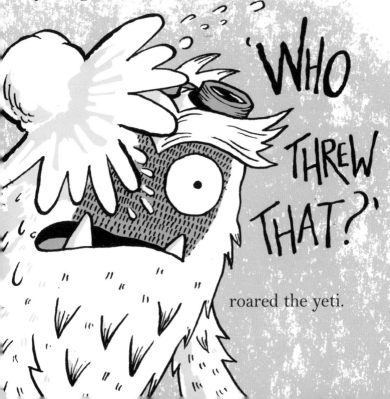

'WHO THREW THAT?'

roared the yeti.

'It was me!' whispered Shen, throwing another snowball.

'It was me!' shouted the snowball, landing on the deck behind the yetis. They all turned to see who had spoken, and Shen whispered, 'Over here!' and threw another.

it called, bursting on the back of the biggest yeti's head.

The biggest yeti turned and glowered at the others.

'It wasn't us!' they said.

said a snowball, landing out of sight in the shadows.

YOU BIG HAIRBALL!

said another.

The biggest yeti pulled some snow
out of his fur and squeezed it into a
snowball. The others scooped snow off
the decks and the roofs of the cabins.
In another moment the air on deck
was full of flying snowballs as the
yetis pelted each other, and Shen kept
throwing snowballs too. 'Missed me!'
Shen's snowballs jeered, and 'Oi, carpet-
features!' and 'Fur-face! Over here!'
And the yetis picked up the burst balls
of echosnow and made fresh snowballs
from them, and the echosnow echoed
their own angry shouts as well as the
things that Shen was whispering.

Before long the snowball fight
had turned into a full-scale
snowball battle.

None of the yetis noticed a small boy scrambling up the side of their old ship and knocking on the kitchen porthole.

The poor washer-uppers inside had not thought to open that porthole. Helga Hammerfest and Mitzi Von Primm and Shackleton Jones could never have squeezed out through it, and Sika was too busy drying up to have even noticed it until Shen started banging on it. She opened it. Shen tumbled in, bringing a cold blast of air with him which startled the washer-uppers to their senses.

'The yetis are having a snowball fight! SNOBOT is waiting with the sleds. We must leave quickly!' He stopped, his mouth hanging open, staring at the grown-ups. Was it just his imagination, or had they changed?

Sika saw it too, now. Helga Hammerfest had always had a beard, but it had not been quite that long before, or quite that soft, and it had not been white.

Shackleton Jones had a white beard now too, and white side whiskers, and bushy white eyebrows. But it was Mitzi Von Primm who had changed most of all. She had put on so much weight that her pink designer racing outfit was starting to split at the seams. Her face and hands were covered with soft white fur, and her eyes glowed blue.

'They're turning into yetis!' said Shen.

'It must be a side-effect of the noodlesnow!' said Sika, and checked her reflection in the bottom of a freshly washed-up saucepan to see if she was turning into a yeti, too. She wasn't, which was a relief. She supposed it must be because the others had all been at the Lost Hope for much longer than her, and they had eaten way more noodles.

'That must be who these yetis are!' she said. 'They are the sailors from the *Hope*, and other poor souls who have happened by, all transformed by eating noodle snow . . .'

'Mmmmm, lovely, lovely noodles,' said Mitzi Von Primm, stroking her own soft white fur.

Shackleton Jones said, 'That is completely impossible! How could anyone turn into a yeti? Most unscientific, I say.' Then he caught sight of his own reflection in the pan which Sika held up in front of him. 'Aaaargh!' he shrieked. 'I don't want to be a yeti!'

'Nor do I,' said Helga. 'There was something I had to do . . . I was on my way to the North Pole . . .'

'Then you'd better get out of here and stop eating noodlesnow!' said Shen.

'But the doors are locked!' complained Sika.

Helga stomped over to the doors and leaned on them with all her weight. There was quite a lot of Helga's weight, and the doors smashed open easily. They all ran out into the ballroom, past the empty table. All except Mitzi, who stopped to pick up a few stray noodles which had fallen on the tablecloth.

'Come on!' shouted Sika.

'And don't eat any more of those!' cried Shackleton Jones.

'But I like them!' said Mitzi, slurping the noodles up. 'And I like being a yeti. Look at my lovely silky fur!' And she shook off the tatters of her ski suit and stretched out her long, white, hairy arms, admiring the way the candlelight shone on her pelt.

'She had more noodles than any of us,' said Helga.

'But Mitzi, what about the race?' asked Shen. 'What about the Snowfather's palace? Don't you want to be the first to reach the top of the world?'

'Oh, you go on without me,' said Mitzi happily. 'I'm going to simply love being a yeti, and I already have my wish—all the lovely noodles I can eat.'

There wasn't really any more that they could do. Mitzi was a proper yeti now, as big as Helga and probably twice as strong, so they could not have dragged her away from the ship. And anyway, she really did seem happy, and it was true, she was a very pretty yeti. So they left her there, and hurried outside to board their sleds, before the rowdy snowball fight on deck ended and the yetis came back below to see if the washing up was finished yet. But just in case Mitzi ever decided she had had enough of yeti-ing, they left her sled behind, and Shackleton Jones left her his robot huskies, and harnessed her team to his hi-tech sled.

'This is SO embarrassing,' said SNOBOT, cracking his whip above the heads of the pink pooches.

'Not as embarrassing as losing the race will be!' called Helga, as her polar bear-powered sled went racing past him. Now that the spell of the noodles had faded, she was remembering how much she wanted to win the race. She waved to Shen and Sika. 'Thanks, kiddies! I'll see you at the top of the world!'

'Jeepers, SNOBOT,' shouted Shackleton Jones, 'let's get moving, or the Bearded Lady will be there before us!'

And pretty soon both their sleds were just dots in the distance, and Shen and Sika were losing the race again.

ELEVEN

The days that followed weren't really days at all; sunrise was just a faint silvering of light upon the southern sky. The pugs ran north as fast as their two hundred and sixty-four little legs could carry them, following the tracks of the other sleds.

There were fifty different types of snow in a True Winter, and Shen and Sika had soon seen nearly all of them.

They crossed patches of blindsnow and patches of echosnow. They plunged through warbling drifts of songsnow

and screaming mounds of
screechsnow. They crossed a
broad, rolling plain of
slumbersnow, which snored and
mumbled and farted like someone asleep
under a huge white eiderdown.

Helga and the rest were so far ahead
now that it barely seemed worth going
on. How could they hope to reach the
North Pole first? But Sika said they
had to try. 'Maybe the other sleds will
all drop out,' she said. 'Or hit a patch
of shrinksnow and be miniaturized, or
a patch of stonesnow and be turned to
statues . . .'

After that, Shen kept a look out for
statues and miniature sleds, but he didn't
see any, just the tracks of the other
racers, leading endlessly on over the
horizon.

They came to a waste of weresnow,
which kept shaping itself into snowmen
when they weren't looking. They would
stop the sled for a while to look at the
compass or cook food on their camping
stove, and look up to find that they
were surrounded by a ring of snowmen.
And these weren't nice snowmen with
scarves, and carrots for noses. Oh no.
These were horrible snowmen with
sharp, icy teeth and frozen claws and
open, hungry mouths.

It was all Very Unsettling.

Before long, Shen and Sika were so tired of being Unsettled that they almost thought of turning back. But the pugs weren't frightened of the weresnow, not even when it tried forming itself into scary snowdogs. They just yipped at them, and eventually some of the braver ones started biting the snowmen's snowy bottoms. After that the weresnow stopped its tricks, though Shen and Sika could still feel it sulking at them as they sped on into the north.

But there was not a lot of north left to speed on into now. Pretty soon they would reach the top of the world, from where, whichever way you go, you're going south. As the last silver smear of the short day faded behind them, they saw something glinting and glittering far ahead. It was the Northern Lights reflecting on the frosty spires of the Snowfather's palace.

Grrrrrr

'We've done it!' said Sika. 'We're nearly there!'

'But I bet one of the others has got there already,' Shen said. He thought that if he kept saying that, it would not be so disappointing if they found that Helga, Shackleton Jones, or Sir Basil was already there. But he could not help hoping, secretly, that Sika was right. They could still be first, if only something had delayed the other racers.

And after a little while longer, when they had crossed a particularly smelly patch of stinksnow, they found that something had.

The Snowfather's palace was not far off now. They could see it sitting there on the horizon like a strange, beautiful crystal. But between them and the palace was a deep chasm. The chasm's walls seemed to reach all the way down

to the floor of the sea. Across
the chasm, like a web of lace,
there stretched a maze of
snow bridges.

'It's beautiful!' said Shen.

'But I'm not sure it can take
our weight . . .' said Sika.

Very slowly, very carefully, they steered the sled on to the first of the bridges. It trembled and creaked, and chunks of snow dropped from its underside and tumbled down into the shadows at the bottom of the abyss. Shen peered down after them and saw spiky white shapes moving down there. Snowtrolls, waiting to eat anyone who fell . . .

'Help!' cried a voice, echoing between the leaping arches and tall, spindly pillars of the snow. The Northern Lights were pulsing brightly overhead, and by their glow the children saw Helga Hammerfest.

Poor Helga! She had done her best to stick to the thickest of the bridges, but even so her mighty bog-oak sled had been too heavy. The middle of one of the bridges had dropped out as she tried to cross it. Her polar bears, Snowdrop and Slushpuppy, sat unhappily on the far side of the gap. The sled, which was still attached to them, dangled in mid-air above the chasm. Helga dangled from the sternpost of the sled. She had tied herself on to it with her beard. From time to time, Snowdrop and Slushpuppy scrambled to their feet

and tried to heave the sled up. It would
rise a few feet, but it was too heavy for
them to drag it back on to the bridge.
Each time they tried, more snow fell
from the bridge, spattering Helga and
her sled and then tumbling on down and
down into the depths.

Shen and Sika looked at each other.
It would have been easy to keep going,
but they could not leave Helga hanging
there.

'Mush!' shouted Shen, and the pugs
surged forwards. Shen and Sika's sled
was so much lighter than Helga's, and
pugs were so much lighter than polar
bears, that even the flimsiest of the
bridges could bear them. They threaded
their way across the maze until they
were on the bit of broken bridge where
Snowdrop and Slushpuppy sat.

'Thank you, children!' Helga shouted,
from down in the blue depths of the

chasm. 'Please cut my poor polar
bears loose. They're getting tired, and I
don't want them to fall along with me.'

'No!' said Shen. 'We're going to pull
you up!'

'Boo!' shouted the snowtrolls, down
in the shadows below. They had been
looking forward to Helga falling, so that
they could eat her. They started hurling
big splinters of ice up at the bridge,
hoping to dislodge her before Shen
and Sika could save her. But the abyss
was deep, and the trolls were rubbish
throwers, so the shards all fell back
harmlessly.

Shen started unhitching the pugs
from Sika's sled and tying their leads to
Snowdrop and Slushpuppy's harnesses.
If the polar bears had been hungry, they
could have eaten the little dogs in sixty-
six big bites, and then had Shen and Sika
for afters. But they were unusually well-

trained polar bears, and they seemed
to understand that Shen and Sika and
all those small, yipping creatures were
there to help.

It took a while, but eventually all the
pugs were attached. 'Mush!' shouted
Sika. The pugs strained forward, pulling
the polar bears. The polar bears
strained forward, pulling the
dangling sled. Inch by inch it
rose, until it was
jammed
against
the

crumbling end of the broken snow
bridge. Then Helga untied her beard
and scrambled up the sled as if
it were a ladder. Gasping
and panting, she heaved
herself up on to
the bridge.
The exhausted
pugs relaxed,
and the sled
dropped again,
dragging polar
bears and pugs
back with it.

Just in time, Helga pulled a big knife from under her furs and slashed through Snowdrop and Slushpuppy's harnesses. The sled dropped silently for a long time, and then, from far below, they heard the deep, echoey crash as it smashed to pieces in the bottom of the chasm. 'Boo!' and 'Spoilsports!' bellowed the trolls, annoyed that nobody had been on it when it fell.

It seemed wrong to leave Helga behind, even though she had left them behind back at the Lost Hope. So they made her sit with Shen on the sled, and Sika went ahead and tested the snow bridges with a stick, while Snowdrop and Slushpuppy walked behind. And they had not gone far when they heard another voice calling, 'Help!'

Shackleton Jones had had the opposite trouble to Helga. He had chosen to cross the maze by the fastest route, across the thinnest and most fragile bridges. He was sure that his super-lightweight sled would not collapse them. But he had forgotten that the pink huskies which were pulling it weighed more than the robot dogs that he had left behind. The frailest of the bridges had crumbled beneath the pink dogs' paws, and now they hung from their harnesses, with only the weight of the sled, Shackleton, and SNOBOT to stop them falling into the chasm. Below them, more hungry trolls were piling up a tower of snow to try and reach the dangling dogs.

'Can you help us, please?' the scientist shouted, when he saw Shen and Sika's sled passing. 'I can't cut these poor doggies loose!'

The trolls' tower was almost tall enough by the time they reached him. A troll climbed to the top of it and, standing on tiptoe, managed to grab the pink pom-pom on one of the dogs' tails. Then it was snatched out of his

156

hand as Shen, Sika, and Helga all helped Shackleton and SNOBOT heave the dogs back on to the bridge.

'Spoilsports!' shouted the trolls.

Shen and Sika went on their way, with Shackleton Jones following. Once or twice he eyed the maze ahead as if he were thinking of ways to get past the children and beat them to the Snowfather's palace, but Helga said, 'Don't even think about it! That's twice those kids have saved us.'

Soon they were nearing the far side of the chasm. And there ahead of them, going carefully across one final bridge, was the sled of Sir Basil Sprout-Dumpling.

TWELVE

Sir Basil looked back and saw the procession that was following him: Sika with her testing stick, the pugs, the pink huskies, the two sleds and two polar bears, Shen, Helga, Shackleton Jones, and SNOBOT.

'Lumme, Sideplate! They've almost caught us up!'

'Indeed, Sir Basil. The crossing of the snow bridges has lost us a great deal of time, sir.'

'Time for some more dirty tricks, Sideplate!'

159

'Oh dear, sir,' said Sideplate.
'Are you sure that's necessary, sir?'
Sir Basil laughed a wicked laugh,
and twirled his moustache, but it had
frozen solid and he snapped the end
off, rather spoiling the effect. Sideplate,
sighing sadly, opened Sir Basil's
expensive antique gun case and lifted
out Sir Basil's expensive antique rocket
launcher.

'I really must protest, Sir Basil,' he said,
as he handed it over. 'Your behaviour
is most unsporting. When we return
to London, I shall be tendering my
resignation, sir.'

'Tender whatever you like, Sideplate,'
sneered Sir Basil, getting the rocket
launcher ready and pointing it at the
snow bridge which the others were just
about to cross. 'I shall have had my wish
granted by then. I'll be the richest man

in the world. I'll be able to hire billions of better butlers than you, you bounder.'

'Very good, sir,' said Sideplate. He winced as Sir Basil pulled the trigger and a rocket went shooting towards the snow bridge.

Sir Basil was a rubbish shot. He had missed the bridge completely! But the rocket hit one of the other bridges, way off at the far side of the chasm. The bridge burst apart and fell into the depths, and the bridge next to it began to crumble too, and then two more bridges which joined on to that. The whole beautiful maze of bridges began to quiver, and sag, and crumble, and collapse.

'Quickly!' shouted Sika, running down the last bridge.

'Quickly, I mean, MUSH!' shouted Shen, urging the pugs after her.

The others followed, as quickly as they dared. Behind them, the final bridge was disintegrating with a rush and a roar of falling snow.

Ahead, Sir Basil was taking aim with another rocket, and this time the travellers were so close that Shen was pretty sure he couldn't miss.

'Take this, you absolute shower!' sneered Sir Basil.

But just as he pulled the trigger, Sideplate's snowboot kicked the rocket launcher upwards. The rocket went whizzing harmlessly off into the sky, to burst some-where among the Northern Lights.

'Sideplate, you spoilsport!' spluttered Sir Basil.

The bridges were still crumbling, filling the air above the chasm with a haze of powdered snow. Sideplate ran to meet Sika and the others as they came spilling on to the ice. The bridge they'd just crossed disintegrated behind them, almost taking Shackleton Jones with it, but he and SNOBOT managed to leap to safety as their sled dropped into the chasm. Helga quickly slashed the pink dogs' harnesses to stop them going with it.

'I must apologize for Sir Basil's behaviour, ladies and gentlemen,' said Sideplate, helping Shackleton Jones climb over the edge of the chasm. 'He has always been a most unsporting gentleman . . .'

'So long, Sideplate!' called Sir Basil, leaping aboard his sled. 'I'll go even faster without you!' His long whip cracked above his huskies' ears, and they started to run towards the far off icicle palace. But just then, with a massive thump, a big, jagged, glowing thing came slamming down, smashing the sled

to pieces and catapulting Sir Bash high
into the air. That last rocket had done
a lot of damage when it exploded up
there among the Northern Lights; now
broken shards of light were dropping
all around, freezing as they plummeted
through the chilly sky.

Shen and his friends waited until the rain of broken lights was over, then they picked their way between the shards to where Sir Basil's sled lay splintered. Sideplate disentangled the dogs, who ran off in all directions woofing happily.

Sir Basil had landed in a deep drift of snow. He scrambled out, shouting more threats and shaking his fist. But his fist seemed smaller than before. All of him did. He was dwindling before their eyes, shrinking down and down until he was no bigger than a toy soldier, while his voice grew higher and higher. 'You beastly blighters! Look what you've made me do! I've fallen into a patch of shrinksnow!'

'Careful!' said Helga, lassoing the tiny cheat with a pug lead. 'We mustn't touch that patch of snow ourselves.'

'If your little dogs got any smaller, we might not be able to see them at all!' said Shackleton Jones.

Helga reeled Sir Basil in, until he was close enough for her to reach out and pick him up. He kept being terribly rude at first, until he realized just how tiny he'd become. Then he said, 'Oh . . . ah . . . no hard feelings, eh?'

'Is there a cure for shrinksnow?' asked Shen.

'I don't know,' said Shackleton Jones. 'The effects may wear off eventually.'

'But I can't stay this size for ever!' wailed Sir Basil. Helga handed him to Sideplate, who put him in a lunch box for safekeeping (making sure to punch some air holes in the lid first). They could hear his tiny, angry voice buzzing in there as they set off again towards the icicle palace.

It wasn't really a race any more; they all just felt that, having come so far, they ought to at least say hello to the Snowfather. There was not enough room on the sled for all of them, so they took turns to walk. It was hard work, crossing that ice, for it was very slippery, and although it had looked flat from the snow bridges, it actually sloped quite steeply upwards.

And as they trudged up that slope, so it grew colder. Shen didn't think it could get any colder, but it did. He had grown used to seeing his breath come out as steam, but here at the top of the world each steamy breath froze solid as soon as he breathed it, and fell on the ice in front of him with a little tinkly sound like a dropped ornament. It was so cold that the pugs, who had run so far and so bravely in their little Aran sweaters, began to shiver, and their tiny feet grew numb, and soon they could barely walk at all. Then Sideplate and Helga gathered them up and Helga wrapped them all in her beard, which was still extravagantly long and white and warm after her meal of yeti noodles. Their little faces peeked out as she plodded onwards, and Sika, Shen, and Shackleton

harnessed the two polar bears and the pink huskies and Sir Basil's dogs to the sled instead.

'Soon it will be too cold to talk,' Shen started to say—but already it was too cold to talk; he decided to keep his mouth shut, in case his tongue froze solid like a pink ice lolly.

And then it was too cold to think. It was as if the ice had got inside his head, and all his thoughts slowed down and stopped, like fish frozen in the sea.

But he kept trudging on, putting one cold foot in front of another, and suddenly he felt the cold ease a little, and then a little more. And he raised his eyes—which had been watching only the ice in front of him— and there was the icicle palace of the

Snowfather towering up into the sky.
From its chimneys, little curlicues
of smoke went up to tangle in the
Northern Lights. And sitting in front
of the high white wall which ran
around the icicle palace, was a
huge old man, bigger even than
Sika's grandpa.

'I'm so glad you made it!' he
said, and his voice was deep
and rich like Christmas
pudding. 'Now, which of
you is the winner?
Whose wish shall I grant?'

THIRTEEN

For a moment, nobody spoke except for Sir Basil, who said, 'Me! I'm the winner of course!' but he was so muffled inside the box that the Snowfather didn't hear him.

In the end, it was Shen who said, 'None of us is the winner. Or we all are.'

'That's true,' said Sika. 'We all got here together, and none of us could have made it without the others. I'd still be washing up for the yetis if SNOBOT hadn't gone and roused Shen . . .'

YIP!

YIP!

'IP!

'We'd all BE yetis if Shen hadn't rescued us,' said Shackleton.

'And I'd have fallen into the chasm if Shen and Sika hadn't helped me,' Helga said.

'And the pugs would have frozen if Helga hadn't nestled them in her beard.'

'And we'd all have been blown up by Sir Basil's rocket if Sideplate hadn't saved us.'

'So none of us is the winner,' said Shen sadly. 'Not really.'

The Snowfather's wide white grin grew wider still. 'Or maybe ALL of you are the winners,' he said. 'For the first time ever, I declare the race a tie. So come inside, and let us discuss the matter of prizes . . .'

They followed him through the gate in the high white wall, into a garden. Green was the last colour they had expected to see here at the top of the world, but green was all around them;

the glowing greens of grass and trees, speckled with red and golden flowers.

'How did you grow all these plants?' asked Shackleton Jones.

'I didn't grow them,' said the Snowfather. 'I made them! Out of snow!'

'Snow?' said Sideplate, reaching out to run his hands over a tree-trunk.

'Everything you see here is made of snow,' said the Snowfather. 'The special anythingsnow that falls only here, at the Top of the World. Shape it into whatever you want, and it will become real.'

He strode over to a drift of snow which had gathered against the wall of his palace. Kneeling, he scooped some up, and made it into a little snow bird. 'There!' he said—and as they watched, the white bird blushed and darkened, opened its black-bead eyes and flittered away to perch singing on the branch of a tree. 'Whatever you like!' he said.

For a moment everyone was
too amazed to speak.

Then, with whoops and cheers, the travellers all threw themselves at that mound of snow, and started to help themselves to clumps of it, and shape those clumps into—well, whatever they could imagine. Shen made a little snow ship, which turned into the most perfect little real ship he had ever seen, complete with rigging and anchor chains and all sorts of things he hadn't been able to sculpt in snow, but which the snow knew he had wanted anyway. He put it in his pocket, and set to work making a snow treasure-chest, and filling it with snowy diamonds.

'Ah, that's what Sir Basil's father did, when he came here all those years ago,' said Sideplate. He was busy making a snow bowler hat, to replace his own, which was looking a bit battered after all his adventures. Meanwhile, Shackleton Jones was making snow cogs and snow wheels, the snowy parts for some snow-machine. And Helga was sculpting a big heap of snow into the shape of a polar bear—which shook itself, roared, and went running off across the lawns to play with Snowdrop and Slushpuppy and the sixty-six pugs. 'You can never have too many friendly polar bears,' said Helga.

And Sika? She just stood and watched, and the Snowfather stood beside her, chuckling at the delight of the others as they busied themselves making snow-things. 'Always the same,' he said. 'Ever since Ooka first came here and discovered the anythingsnow.'

'What did she make?' asked Sika.

'Ah,' said the Snowfather, 'she was feeling rather lonely, having come so far all by herself, so she made a snowman. She didn't even know it was anythingsnow she was making him from, but she lay down to sleep beside him, and when she woke up . . .'

'He had come alive?' asked Sika.

The Snowfather smiled and nodded, remembering.

'And what about you, young Sika?' he asked. 'What will you make?'

'I don't know,' said Sika. 'The thing I want isn't a thing. I came here to ask if you could make my grandpa better.'

'Oh my dear,' said the Snowfather gently. 'I'm afraid that is a bit beyond me.'

'But you grant wishes, don't you? That's what all the stories say. They say you'll give the winner their heart's desire.'

'I think there's been a bit of a mix-up, then,' said the Snowfather. 'I am the guardian of the anything snow, but I cannot grant wishes. If people have got their heart's desire by coming here, then either their heart's desire was something they could make out of snow, or it was something which they found along the way, like your grandpa did.'

'Do you remember my grandpa?'

'Of course I do! Such a brave boy he was. I hoped he'd win, but Sir Basil's father beat him in the end (I suspect Sir Basil's father was a cheat, like his son). But it did not matter! Your grandpa didn't need to fill his pockets with snow-jewels. Just the journeying here was prize enough for him; just to see all the wonders of True Winter, and go home with stories to tell.'

'Such stories!' said Sika. 'And when he dies, there will be no more.'

'No, no,' said the Snowfather. 'All old things die in the end, but not stories. Stories go on and on, and new ones are always being born. Now, join the others, before the snow is all used up.'

So Sika ran to join Shen who had finished his chest of snow-diamonds and was now busy making sixty-six snow bones for the sixty-six pugs. Sika helped, and while she was at it she thought of a few things which she had always wanted too, and together they made those out of snow.

And then everyone remembered how hungry they were, and they started making snow-food which they carried inside and ate in a huge feast beside the Snowfather's roaring snow-log fire. And while they ate, they all talked about what they were going to do next.

'I've got my wish,' said Shackleton Jones. 'SNOBOT has collected enough data and enough samples of these strange types of snow that I'll be kept busy for years. I'll be famous! I'll probably get a snowflake named after me. And I'm going to call in at the Lost Hope on my way home.

It seems to me that what those yetis really need is an electric dishwasher, and I'm just the man to make it for them.'

'I'm going to buy Sir Basil's stately home,' said Sideplate, 'and settle down and live there. If Sir Basil grows back to normal size I shall let him stay on as my butler. If not, he can move into one of the houses on my model train set.'

'Humph,' said Sir Basil, grumpily. (He was sitting on a matchbox on the table, nibbling at a peanut, which was the size of a roast turkey to him.) 'If it hadn't been for you interfering rotters I'd have won the race and been the richest man in the world, not the titchiest.'

'Oh, but you were always a small man,' said the Snowfather. 'Inside, you were always a tiny little man. You have just shrunk to fit yourself.'

'The houses on my model train set are very nice,' said Sideplate, encouragingly. 'You can settle down there, sir. And you'll certainly be the richest man in that world, so, in a way, you will have got your wish.'

'Well, I'm going to settle down too,' said Helga Hammerfest, who had talked quietly and seriously with the Snowfather while the others were still eating. 'I'm going to stay right here. That's my wish. It's the perfect place for polar bears, and for me too. There was never enough winter in the world for my liking.'

'What about you, Shen?' asked the Snowfather. 'What's your wish?'

'I'm going to take all those diamonds back to Snowdovia and buy a fantastic new ship,' said Shen. But now that he had the money to buy a ship, he felt a bit sad about it. He would be sorry to sail away from Sika. And when he looked at Sika he felt even sadder, because although she had a nice new snow-made hat and things, she hadn't come all this way for those—she had come so that the Snowfather could save her grandpa, and that was the one thing the Snowfather couldn't do.

After the feast they slept—a good night's sleep in white beds as deep and soft as snowdrifts. And when they woke, it was time to go home. Out in the Snowfather's gardens, Sideplate was strapping Sir Basil's lunchbox firmly to his sled, with Sir Basil buzzing inside it like a posh wasp. Shackleton Jones was preparing his own sled for take-off—he had fitted it with wings and propellers which he had made out of snow, and he was being helped by SNOBOT, and by a new robot called SNOBOT 2 whom SNOBOT had made out of snow.

Helga was walking in the Snowfather's garden, watching her polar bears play on the lawn. 'This is the place for me,' she said happily. 'Ever since I was a little girl, I've wanted to come here, and to stay. No more dreary springs and summers for me. Winter is best. Winter glitters.'

Shen and Sika went to where they had left Grandpa's sled. It was looking rather the worse for wear after its long journey. The leads which tied the pugs to it were tattered and frayed.

'It's a long way for small paws,' said the Snowfather, watching while they started arranging the little dogs.

That was true. The pugs did not look happy at the thought of the long journey that lay ahead. 'But we have to go,' said Sika. 'It's lovely here, but we don't want to stay for ever, like Helga.' Then she looked at the Snowfather and said, 'I've been thinking, about my wish . . .'

'You know I cannot give you your heart's desire,' said the Snowfather.

'I know,' she said. 'But could you maybe give my grandpa his heart's desire instead?'

'And what would that be?'

'To see you, one more time,' said Sika.

The Snowfather went quiet and thoughtful for a while. While he was thinking, Shackleton Jones's sled went soaring overhead, with Shackleton and the SNOBOTs waving from the windows. It circled the icicle palace once, and roared away into the south-west.

'That's the only way to travel,' said the Snowfather approvingly, shading his eyes to watch the flying sled as it dwindled among the Northern Lights. He turned and ran back into his garden, to a fresh fall of anything snow which had appeared overnight. Shen and Sika stood watching while he began shaping the snow into six big shapes. When he was finished, six huge elk shook themselves to life, and started nibbling the grass while the Snowfather made six red harnesses for them and led them outside to where Shen and Sika's sled was waiting.

'Your dogs have run further than any pugs ever ran before,' he said, as he started tying the elk to the sled. 'It would be a pity to make them run all the way back again, too!'

There was barely enough room on the sled for Shen and Sika and the Snowfather and Shen's snow treasure-chest and sixty-six pugs, but they all squeezed on somehow. When everyone was aboard, the Snowfather shouted something to his elk, and off they set, galloping across the snow with the sled rushing behind them, until the hiss of the sled's runners suddenly faded, and Shen looked over the side and saw that they were flying. The elk had unfolded great tawny wings and were flapping southwards. The Snowfather's palace in its green ring of gardens was falling away below, with Helga Hammerfest waving, and Sideplate looking up and waving too, as he set out on his own journey.

Shen waved back, but pretty soon the sled was so high that he did not think they could see him any more. He could see them, though. He could see everything; the icicle palace and the abyss with its broken bridges, and the fifty different kinds of snow. He could see, far away, the Lost Hope, and, further still, Kraken Deep and the Dark Forests where the pugs' yipping had shaken down those dumps of snow. He could see all the wideness and whiteness of the frozen north, spread out under the Northern Lights like a map, or the iced top of a gigantic Christmas cake.

The Snowfather laughed, and tugged on the elks' reins, and the sled flew south, towards the far-away, twinkling windows of Snowdovia.

FOURTEEN

It was midnight at the Po of Ice and Grandpa lay dreaming. His bed was a sled again, carrying him over the shining ice, under the glimmering green canopies of the Northern Lights.

Suddenly, he opened one eye. Was that wings he'd heard? Passing across the sky above the shop, settling on the snow outside . . .

Somewhere a door opened, quiet as quiet. A breath of cold stole into the warm room. The tiny sounds of tiptoe feet on floorboards.

Grandpa opened the other eye. 'I thought you were a dream,' he said.

'I'm not,' said the Snowfather, filling the room like a kindly shadow, stooping to fit his bigness under the slope of the ceiling.

'Then is my bed really a sled?' asked Grandpa. 'Am I at the top of the world again?'

'No,' said the Snowfather. 'I have come south, for a change. Helga Hammerfest and her bears will keep an eye on things at the Pole while I'm away. Sika tells me that you wanted to see me again.'

'I wanted to come to you,' said Grandpa. 'I wanted to make that journey one last time. But I know I'm too old now for journeys. I shall make do with the stories of Sika's journey, instead.'

'And I've got such stories to tell!' she said, and she climbed up on to the bed to put her arms around Grandpa's neck. 'So many adventures, such things we've seen, me and Shen!'

And they started to tell him. The Snowfather stood listening, and after a while Sika's mum came in, woken by the voices. And there they all sat, the whole night long, while the Northern Lights shone in very brightly through the windows, and Grandpa and Sika and Shen and the Snowfather swapped their stories.

And towards morning, Grandpa fell asleep, still smiling at the memories of the things they'd told him. Deeper and deeper he sank into his dreams, and the sound of his snoring grew more and more faint, until at last it faded altogether, and they knew that he would not wake up.

They were sad and silent for a while, until the Snowfather said, 'Come.'

'Come where?' asked Sika's mother.

The Snowfather opened the door on the far side of Grandpa's bedroom. The cold came into the room. He went round behind Grandpa's bed and started to push it towards the open door. Shen and Sika ran to help—they did not know why he was pushing the bed outside, but they were sure he must have a good reason. After a moment, Sika's mum joined in too. Together, the four of them eased the bed outside. It looked even more like a sled, standing there on the glittering snow.

The Snowfather stooped and scooped up a handful of the snow. He looked at it, and smiled. 'I thought so!' he said.

'What is it?' they asked.

'It is my favourite of all the fifty kinds of snow,' he said.

He breathed on the clump of snow that was in his hand, and it came apart in soft white flakes. The flakes drifted into the air like loose feathers from an eiderdown. It took Shen a moment to realize what was strange about them.

'They're falling upwards!' he said.

The flakes were too light to go straight up—every breath of air blew them off course—but they were definitely rising. And all across the snowy yard outside the Po of Ice, more flakes were lifting, detaching themselves from the drifts and banks and whispering softly up into the night.

Like a blizzard in reverse, the upward-falling snow poured up into the night, and the snow that was under Grandpa's bed caught

against the slats
and the underneath of
the mattress and kept
rising, so that the bed

was lifted with it,
turning and trembling like a
boat that feels the tug of the tide.

'Where is it going?' asked Sika.

'He's going on that one last journey
that he always wished for,' said her
mother.

'That's right,' said the Snowfather.
'He's going to places even I have never
seen.'

'Goodbye, Grandpa!' Sika whispered.
Up and up the wild snow fell, a
column of dancing flakes like the sparks
from a cold fire, with the bed borne
in the heart of it. Up and up, slowly
dwindling into the heights of the sky,
where the Northern Lights danced so
brightly. Shen and Sika and Sika's mum
joined hands and watched it go. The
Snowfather watched with them for a
little while. Then he went back to where
his sled was waiting.

Shen and Sika and her mum stood and
watched the bed as it faded into the
heights of the sky. Long after the bed
was lost to sight, Shen and Sika,
and her mum still stood there,
staring after it.

The last flakes of the upside-down
blizzard fluttered up around them,
leaving the ground around the Po
of Ice with only a thin covering of
ordinary snow. And suddenly Shen felt
very lonely, because he knew that his
adventure was almost over, and that
soon it would be time to leave this place.

But then, as if she knew how he was
feeling, Sika's mum put her hand on his
shoulder and said, 'I've been thinking,
Shen. I think, if you want to, that you
should stay here, you and your sixty-
six pugs. I mean to open the Po of Ice
properly again, and start a hot chocolate
cafe, and rent out rooms to people who
come to see the Northern Lights.'

Then Shen knew what his heart's
desire had been all along. Not a new
ship; a new life, here in this cozy old,
snowy old post office.

'I can help!' he said. 'We could start a
pug-powered parcel delivery service!

And we'll use the treasure from the Snowfather's garden to pay for a new roof, and a new S and T and F . . .'

'Oh!' said Sika suddenly. 'The Snowfather!'

They ran to where the sled had been. There on the snow in a sleepy heap, sixty-six pugs snuggled under a pile of furs and blankets. There stood Shen's treasure chest, and the other treasures they had brought back with them. But the sled was gone, and the Snowfather with it, back to his home at the North Pole.

'He didn't even say goodbye,' said Shen.

'He didn't need to,' said Sika.

In the silence of the night they heard a soft drip-drip-drip.

The fringe of icicles which draped the eaves of the Po of Ice were weeping meltwater tears.

'There's a change in the weather coming,' said Sika's mother.

'True Winter is going away,' said Sika, sadly. 'It'll just be an ordinary winter now, and then spring again. There won't be another True Winter for a whole lifetime.'

But Shen didn't feel sad. Because at least he'd seen all those things; the Kraken and the yetis and the fifty different kinds of snow. At least he'd gone to the top of the world and met the Snowfather. And now he was going to live here, in this strange place, among these funny, stilty houses. He was going to come to know these hills and woods and fjords in all their different seasons, all their different moods. And maybe, when a lifetime had passed and True Winter returned, he'd meet the Snowfather again.

But until then . . .

. . . until then . . .

. . . what a lifetime it was
going to be!

ABOUT THE AUTHORS

When **PHILIP REEVE** was little, his family had a black long-haired Chihuahua named Nero, who loved going hillwalking. Nero climbed most of Britain's highest mountains, including Snowdon, Helvellyn and Scafell Pike, and everybody he met on the way up said 'I bet his legs were longer when he started.' It was quite funny the first time.

He lives on Dartmoor with his wife Sarah, their son Sam, a poodle and two alpacas.

Philip and Sarah came up with ideas together for this book, then Philip wrote the words and Sarah drew the pictures. Since they're good friends, they helped each other along the whole way.

When **SARAH McINTYRE** was 16, she climbed Mount Rainier with her dad and his buddies. Her favourite part of hiking on snow is 'glissading', which means sliding down a hill on your bum, using an ice axe as a brake. She has never had a dog, but now she has 66, all in this book. She lives in London with her husband, Stuart.

Meh.

visit us at www.facebook.com/reeveandmcintyre